THE HOTEL NAMED STARLIGHT

A PARANORMAL DEMONIC HAUNTED HOTEL NOVEL

SIDDHARTH NAHAL

This book is dedicated to my family and friends who have always supported me in all of my ventures.

Contents

Preface

This is a special book, not only because it's the first book I ever wrote but also because this is based on the very first short story I wrote. On 4th August 2021, I wrote a short story titled "Hotel Starlight." The response I received for that story was good enough to encourage me to keep on writing. On 29th August 2021, I wrote another short story that was a continuation of Hotel Starlight. When I was thinking about what horror story to write as my first book, it occurred to me that I should start my book writing journey with the same story that developed my passion for writing. Both of the short stories this story is based on are included exactly as I wrote them in this book. I genuinely hope that you enjoy reading this.

*The characters and events portrayed in this book are fictitious. Any similarity to real persons, living or dead, is coincidental and not intended by the author.

CHAPTER ONE

"The days are so much more hectic now. I think we need to hire more people." I said as I took the dish from the chef. "Table number 3, please. You know that boss is not hiring anybody else here, so it's just you, me, and him till the very end." The chef replied. After delivering the dish to table number 3, I sat down and drank a glass of water. Just then, the landline phone that we used for taking orders for home delivery rang. I picked it up and said, "Moonshine kitchen, how may I help you?" From the other end, a man's voice said, "I would like to order two burgers and fries. Deliver it to Hotel Starlight, room number 4." To this, I responded, "Sir, could you please tell me the complete address?" the man immediately said, "I am just a traveler; I don't know the entire address. Use that thing on your mobile phone that shows you locations; umm, what is it called again? Yeah, goggle maps. Use that and find your way here, and please be quick. I WILL BE WAITING." There was something unnatural feeling in the man's voice as he said the last line, but I ignored it and gave the chef the order, thinking it must just be some glitch due to a weak network.

As I was listening to the orders from the customers sitting in the restaurant, the only thing running through my mind was the weird man who had ordered food. All I could think of was the way he had talked about google maps (and called it goggle maps for some reason), which is very useful and popular these days. He referred to it as if he had never used it or even heard of it before. "What a weird person." I thought to myself as I served food at a table. Just then, I heard the chef call me. I finished serving the food and went straight to the kitchen, where the food was packed and ready to be delivered. I told him to take care of the orders that came in and immediately left to deliver the food. I went and sat on my bike, opened google maps, and searched for hotel starlight. Every single time I searched for it, the screen flashed with the following message: *No results found.*

On the fourth try, one location popped up. When I clicked on it, the google page of the hotel opened. The thing that was unnatural was that there were beautiful images of an exquisite-looking building, every other required information from timing to contact details and over twenty thousand reviews. I thought this was a new hotel or something, but I didn't know that this was an already established place that was quite popular. "How come I never heard of it?" I said out loud. "Maybe because you don't do your work properly because of which we are not getting orders from anywhere." I sighed and turned around. There stood Garry, the owner of the restaurant I worked at. Garry was a short, chubby man with short hair and a high-pitched voice, which, honestly, was very painful for regular human ears. "Hello, boss. I was just going out to deliver an order to hotel starlight. Any idea where it is?" Garry said, "Am I the person supposed to deliver the order or you? Figure it out and do it fast." I could clearly hear the anger in his shrill voice, so I started my bike, along with the navigation to hotel Starlight on google maps, and immediately left.

I was about to reach the location when my bike stopped working. I got off the bike to take a look at what happened but couldn't find anything wrong with it. Since I was getting late for the delivery and I was close to the location, I decided to go on foot, leaving my bike by the side of the empty road. As I walked towards the location, looking at google maps to find my way there, I reached an empty street, with no cars or people within visible range, but a row of houses to the left, among which there stood a very tall building with a huge neon signboard that had HOTEL STARLIGHT written on it in big blue lettering. I entered the building and was absolutely shocked at what I saw. Among the row of old, worn-out houses, there stood a beautiful and exquisite-looking, extravagant five-star hotel that just looked as beautiful from the outside as it did from the inside. I was not sure how to react to any of this. I still couldn't believe that I did not know about such a place's existence. I moved towards the reception slowly, admiring everything I saw. The receptionist looked at me and asked, "What can I help you with, sir?" I responded, "I have an order here for room number four." The receptionist looked at me, smiled, and then said, "I believe you can go up to the room, sir, and deliver the food yourself to room number four on the first floor. The guest staying in room number four has been anticipating your arrival." All I could think about was that this receptionist talked as weirdly as the man who had called to place an order earlier. "Thank you," I said. "I will just deliver this and come."

As soon as I said this, "I turned around and walked straight to the stairs. The 30-second conversation that took place was the most awkward and weird conversation I had ever been a part of. I immediately ran up the stairs and started looking at room numbers, and finally, I had found my destination, ROOM NUMBER FOUR. I pressed the bell button that was present on the wall right next to the door and heard a faint 'Ding Dong' sound come from inside. I stood there for five minutes but nobody opened the door. I pressed the bell again, but nobody answered. Finally, I knocked on the door twice, and on the second knock, the door opened slightly on its own. As I pushed the door open, a feeling of uneasiness took over me. I could not believe for a second what I had seen.

CHAPTER TWO

I slowly stepped inside the room, and as the whole room came into view, my jaw dropped. This room looked nothing like the rest of the hotel. Where the rest of the hotel looked like a recently built, well-kept, 5-star hotel, this room looked ancient. This room was so different from the rest of the hotel that it felt as if I had traveled back in time. The walls were covered in spider webs and dust, there was a thick layer of dust on the floor, bugs crawling everywhere, and the room had a very ancient design and looked like a room from a king's palace. It had beautiful artwork covering the walls, which were now covered in spider webs. It looked as if the room had been closed shut for thousands of years. There wasn't any furniture kept in the room. The sound of each step echoed in this empty, ancient room. I was so confused that I did not know what to do. I kept the parcel of food down on the ground as questions filled my head. WAS I HALLUCINATING? Confused and unaware of what to do or think, I decided to leave the room immediately. As I turned around to leave, I was shocked at what I saw. There was no door there anymore. JUST A DUST-COVERED, ANCIENT WALL.

"What is happening?" I said as I was starting to feel a little scared. I looked around the room as confusion and fear took over me completely, and I started to panic. Another weird thing to note was that the room didn't have any form of light in it, but everything in there was very clearly visible. I don't know why this thought came to my mind at that moment, but it could have been the fear making me go crazy and think about this at such a critical time. As I looked around the room for an exit, panic took over me entirely, and I sat down on the ground, thinking that I would be trapped in this doorless, windowless room for eternity.

Just at that moment, I heard a loud hissing noise coming from the other end of the room. I got up as soon as I saw what was making that sound. There was a giant snake, at least 20 feet long, looking straight towards me, coiling up, ready to strike at the first move I make. I stood there, shaking with fear, thinking about all the decisions that led me up to this moment. "I will not work at that stupid restaurant when I manage to get out of here. Just because of that place, I am stuck in this situation. But will I be able to get out? This snake will surely eat me whole. What do I do? is this all a bad dream? Maybe I should just close my eyes and open them again, and all this would be gone." My chain of thought was all over the place, but I knew that this wasn't a dream. It was all happening to me in real life. At that moment, I noticed that there was a door right behind the snake. That had to be my way out of here. As five minutes passed with me standing still, trying to figure out how to get to the door without dying, I decided that I needed to do something to get out of there. Naturally, I started moving towards the door slowly, trying my level best not to make a sound that might startle the snake in any way. The snake's head moved with every little step of mine, its eyes still fixated on me as I moved towards the door. YES! Finally, I had reached the door. Just then, my phone started to ring. "Oh no," I said out loud as I looked at the snake that opened its mouth, ready to strike at me.

Without thinking about it, I reached for the door handle and grabbed it, still looking at the snake that had launched itself straight at my ankle. I yelled in pain as the snake dug its long fangs straight into my ankle, and my hand got burnt entirely because I hadn't noticed that the door handle was glowing red and was at least 500 degrees hot, or so it felt like it. I fell to the floor, squirming in pain, as the snake took another shot at my arm, digging its fangs deep into my forearm. I lay there, screaming in pain with my eyes closed, praying for it to get over soon as I was aware that the snake's venom was spreading fast throughout my body. I wasn't able to feel my leg anymore, and my arm was starting to get numb. My throat grew dry, and I knew that I didn't have much longer. The pain in my burnt hand increased as every second passed. As I lay there, I could feel the warm tears flowing down my cheek, and it became harder to breathe as every second passed by. Suddenly, I realized that something was weird. It had all stopped. No more snake hissing and no more pain. WAS THIS IT? WAS I DEAD?

I slowly opened my eyes. The room looked exactly the same, except there was no snake this time, but the door with the burning hot handle was still there. I looked down at my hand and was surprised to see that it was perfectly fine. I glanced at the door's handle and saw that it was not red anymore. I slowly approached the door, scared to touch the handle. As I got closer to it, I started sweating profusely. Fear slowly grew in me as I approached the once red-hot door handle. I slowly and cautiously touched it, ready to pull my hand back immediately if it was still as hot as before. Luckily, it didn't burn me, but it did something worse this time. As soon as I knew it was safe, I grabbed the handle. Just as I was about to turn it, I heard a loud clanking noise; it sounded like metal keys clanking against each other. Exactly at that moment, I felt a sharp pain run through my skull, and I saw something that scared me to such an extent that I started shivering.

CHAPTER THREE

I could clearly see the corridor right outside the unusual room I was in. There was a man standing right at the very end of the corridor, which had a hinged keyring in his hand, carrying what looked like at least 70-80 identical keys. What scared me entirely was the man's appearance. The corridor was not too long, so I could clearly see him, and as soon as I did, everything felt gloomy. It felt as if all the life, colors, and happiness had been taken out of the world, and now only sorrow and gloom prevailed. The feeling of sadness took over me, and all I could think about was that my end was near. The man standing at the end of the corridor wore an old-fashioned, torn-up blue suit; the hair on his head was in patches and looked partially burnt. His face was an even more horrific site to look at. His nose was weirdly chipped off, exposing his nose bone. He didn't have lips, just a series of vertical stitches that made it appear as if he was smiling. The hand with which he held the keys was burnt up to the elbow. He had a broken bone sticking out of his right thigh that tore through the old, ragged suit.

Just looking at him made me sick to my stomach. He stood there, absolutely still. Suddenly, the man was standing almost an inch away from me. I could feel the warm air coming out of his nose or whatever was remaining of it hit my face. The smell was so bad that I gagged. After a few seconds, the man decided to move. He brought his hand, now holding a bright red key, close up to my face, and as soon as the key touched my forehead, I winced with pain. I could feel a warm, thick liquid pour down my cheek and hit the ground. I was bleeding from my forehead. Pain filled my head as I felt my head throbbing. I looked down as I winced with pain and saw that there was no blood on the floor. In fact, the floor wasn't the same as the floor of the corridor. I looked up and saw that I was back in room number 4. I was just standing there looking at the wall. "WHERE DID THE DOOR GO?" I said as I looked around slowly. I suddenly realized that my head was not bleeding anymore. There was no pain. WHAT WAS GOING ON IN THIS PLACE?

At that moment, the only thought that came to my mind was that I had to get out of there. I started looking around and saw that there was the original door that I had entered through earlier, wide open. I ran out of the room immediately and into the beautiful corridor of the supposed 5-star hotel called HOTEL STARLIGHT, where I didn't know what in the world was going on. As I ran towards the stairs, something made me stop dead in my tracks. in the room I was in front of at that moment, room number 2, there were about 15 to 20 people floating in the air. Yes, FLOATING. I entered the room and saw that all of them were entirely pale. THEY WERE ALL DEAD, but there was something else also. Two people were tied up in the back-left corner of the room, squirming and trying their best to free themselves. They saw me and tried to call out to me through their covered mouths. It was very disturbing to look at. Their eyes were begging me to free them as they tried to scream and call out to me for help. As I looked at them, I saw a glimpse of the weird man again.

He was standing right behind them and looking straight at me with his lifeless, empty eyes. I blinked, and he was gone. Just then, I realized that all the bodies were staring at something. Their eyes were fixated on the wall right in front of them. I turned around to see what it was and saw my name on the wall, written in bold red letters.

DAVID

As soon as I saw that, chills ran down my spine. I turned to look at the people tied up and whispered, "I am so sorry," and without wasting a single second, I ran straight out of the room and down the stairs. I was entirely shaking with fear as I ran out of the hotel. As I got out, I looked back and saw the weird man standing there in the window, which, if I had to guess, was room number 4. I immediately got onto my bike and drove off as fast as I could. Flashes of all the dead bodies and that weird man, or whatever that was, kept coming back to me. I tried my best not to think about anything, but the memory of the snake incident and everything else had definitely left me in a trauma. I just knew where I had to go, the police station.

I reached the police station and immediately went up to the police officer standing right outside the main entrance to the station and said, "Ma'am, the hotel....... dead bodies...... something is wrong........ please help." I was so scared that I wasn't even able to say a single sentence correctly. She looked at me and said, "My name is officer Lauren. Please Calm down, take a deep breath, come inside the station and tell me what or who are you so scared of that you are not able to speak properly." I looked at her and said, "There is no time to sit. There are two inn.....innocent people who have been held captive, but I don't know by who. Please take a few officers to hotel star.......starlight immediately." She looked at me, absolutely confused.

"There is no hotel named starlight in this town. Are you sure about the name?" I didn't understand anything that was happening and therefore blurted out, "Of course, I am sure about the name. I worked at a small restaurant and had gone there to deliver food when unnatural things started happening with me." Then I told her everything that happened with me and all that I saw at that place, and all I saw was the utter look of disbelief on her face. I was sure that SHE DID NOT BELIEVE ME AT ALL. Why is it that people only believe what they see? Anyways, from this awkward conversation, I was sure that all this was just a waste of time, but then something unexpected happened. The police officer said, "I don't know about all that, but you said there were two people tied up. I have never heard about this place, but I will take two officers with me to investigate. Just take us to the location quickly." I was definitely not expecting this to happen, but I had to show them all what I saw, so we headed to the hotel starlight.

CHAPTER FOUR

I took the officers to the place where hotel starlight was located, and throughout the drive there, I could not stop thinking about the two people I saw tied up, hoping that they were fine, but the fear at the back of my head was increasing as the thought that that man or whatever it was, might have converted them to floating bodies. On the way there, my phone kept ringing. It was Garry. Everything happening was so confusing and hard to explain that I didn't pick up the call and dropped a message that said- "I am feeling a bit under the weather currently. I have made the delivery at hotel starlight and am headed back to my apartment. Will be there tomorrow morning." I knew that I might end up losing my job, but if it helped save someone's life, I didn't mind. (Also, texting while riding a bike is definitely not easy or safe.) As we reached there, I stopped my bike right in front of the building. The police car stopped exactly behind me. As all the officers got out, Officer Lauren looked at me and asked, "Where is it?"

I pointed towards the beautifully crafted hotel building. she looked at me and said, "Do you think it is funny to waste the time of the police?" I could hear the anger building up in her voice. "I could arrest you right now for wasting the time of three police officers and playing some stupid prank on the police." I could clearly feel that she wasn't joking (I am not sure as to why she would, but after all that I had seen today, it didn't seem absurd.) I was entirely confused. I immediately asked, "What are you talking about? I am not joking about anything. Now hurry, you need to go inside the hotel and check all the rooms on the first floor, and remember, DO NOT ENTER ROOM NUMBER FOUR." She looked at me furiously and said, "ENOUGH! We will leave now, and I am warning you that if you play a prank like this ever again, I will make sure that you are put in jail for at least a few months." In utter confusion, I blurted out, "What prank are you talking about? The hotel is right in front of you, and what I said about the bodies and the people in danger will also be true if you will just go in and check. I know what I saw. It can't be a hallucination or anything else. Please, just please once, go in and see for yourself." As I was looking at her, almost about to cry, she told me to turn around and look at the hotel, and I did as I was told to. I looked at the hotel, and it looked exactly how it had looked two minutes ago. I didn't understand why she told me to look at it again. Just then, she said, "What hotel, huh? You need to see a doctor as something is terribly wrong with you. Can't you see, THERE IS NO HOTEL THERE. Just an empty piece of land."

As soon as I heard that, I immediately turned to look at her. "Wh...what?!" I exclaimed. "What do you mean that there is no hotel? It's.... it's right there. IT IS RIGHT THERE. I can clearly see it." I pointed straight at the building and started waving my hand up and down in a continuous motion. "How is it possible that I see it and you don't?" As I said this, she looked at me, with pity clearly visible in her eyes, and said, "come by the station tomorrow, and I will give you the details of a good doctor that can help you with whatever problem you are dealing with. Right now, just go home and take some rest." The other two officers looked at me as if they didn't care about anything and just wanted to get out of there. After a very long minute of awkward silence, the officers had left, and I still stood there, right next to my bike, trying to compute everything that had happened, and the worst part of it all was that none of it made any sense. I turned around and looked at the hotel building again as I got back on my bike, still thinking. As I started my bike and was about to leave, I saw him again. Standing behind the tall, clear, glass window, looking straight into my eyes with his empty and lifeless ones. I knew staying there was not a good idea, so I left, still thinking about all that had happened. I had already taken the day off, and it was starting to get dark as the night approached, so I went straight home to get some rest. After all, it had been a hectic day.

CHAPTER FIVE

I reached home in about half an hour, and as soon as I entered my house, a feeling of fear took over me. All the lights in the apartment were switched off, and it was pitch black. I immediately turned on all the lights and went into the bathroom. It was when I looked into the mirror I realized that I was sweating profusely. I was pretty sure at this point that I had been scarred forever by the incident that had happened, but now that I was home, I FELT SAFE. I sat down on the old, tattered couch in my living room and checked my phone, there were multiple messages from Garry asking what had happened, and the last message was what shocked me. It said that he was coming over to my place to check on me. I knew something was wrong. You see, Garry has never been the kind of person to really care about anyone, especially his employees. I tried calling him but got no response. I even left messages, but he did not respond or even see them.

I got up and went straight to my bedroom and sat down on the bed for a while surfing through my phone, thoughts of everything that took place today still racing through my head. Another long hour passed with me trying to distract myself from the thoughts about the weird hotel, for which I tried watching videos, surfing the internet, and even sleeping, all in vain. Whenever I closed my eyes and tried to sleep, I could clearly see it. The weird man standing there, bearing a creepy smile made out of vertical stitches, looking straight into my eyes. His gaze piercing straight through to my soul, sending shivers down my spine. It always ended with me opening my eyes, looking straight at the roof, and sweating. When nothing was working, I felt that I needed more information on that place; I just needed to know, so, as curiosity took over me, I sat up on my bed, picked up my phone, and went on google. I was just about to search for information on hotel starlight when the doorbell rang.

I got up, went to the door, and looked through the peephole. There was no one out there. "Someone must be playing a prank," I thought, but as soon as I turned around to head back to my room, the bell rang again. I immediately turned back towards the door and looked through the peephole. Nobody was visible. The entire corridor stood there, completely empty. I was starting to get annoyed now. As I decided to ignore it and go back to my room, the bell rang again. This made me angry. I opened the door and said, "Enough of the stupid joke!" But this time, the corridor was not empty. Garry stood there, looking at me, confused but somewhat irritated. "What are you talking about, David? What joke? I just came by to see how you were holding up. Didn't you get my messages?" He said as he looked at me with eyes that almost looked lifeless. The way in which he spoke felt very strange. It did not sound like him at all. "Ya..... Yeah, Garry, I am fine. Just a little bit under the weather. What about you? Are you doing fine? You sound a bit sick" to this, Garry responded, "Nothing at all, just a bit tired." it was weird, but I ignored it and said, "Sorry for making you stand here, please come in." he entered, and I told him to sit while I made coffee for him.

I went into the kitchen, and as I started preparing the coffee, I heard Garry ask something that I didn't know how to answer. He asked, "David, what did you think about HOTEL STARLIGHT? Beautiful, isn't it? A one-of-a-kind creation." His voice sounded different, as if something was stuck in his throat that muffled his voice and led to the words not coming out properly, which made his voice sound very broken and cracked. I continued to make the coffee and replied, "Are you okay, Garry? Your voice sounds a bit different. Do you need water?" For an entire minute, there was such a strong silence that I felt something was wrong. I asked, "Garry, is everything alright? The coffee is almost ready. Do you need anything else?" As I poured the coffee into the only two fancy plastic mugs I had, both of which I only used when guests came over, I could hear a faint whisper say, "All I wanted was to live, David. Look what your little adventure at the beautiful hotel did to me. YOU ARE RESPONSIBLE FOR THIS! You are the one who took that order which could have been avoided, but you took it anyway. You could have prevented all this, David, but now you have set him free by going into room number 4 and now look what he did to me. TURN AROUND, DAVID, LOOK AT ME! LOOK WHAT YOU DID!" As soon as I heard this, I spun around to see Garry standing in the doorway to my kitchen. His condition made me gag. I couldn't look at him. It was horrendous. You could see his bright pink flesh in many places of his body, skin hanging freely from those areas, about to fall. He had a long blade going right through the center of his throat. Half of his arm was burnt, and his hand was weirdly closed as if he was holding something in it, but I was certain that it was empty. In his broken voice, Garry said, "Your end is inevitable, David. He is coming for you. You cannot escape him. You cannot hide from him. He will destroy everything!" streams of blood came out of his mouth as he said these words, looking straight at me, with eyes full of fear. I looked at him with confusion and disgust as sweat poured down my forehead due to the immense fear I felt. The feeling that filled me next was something I recognized very easily. It was the same feeling of sorrow and gloom that I felt when I saw that weird man for the first time earlier today. I immediately asked him, "Who is coming? Who is he? The weird man from that hotel?" He looked at me with fear. Suddenly, he started shaking and fell to the floor. I ran up to him, and I could hear him whisper as he breathed his last. He kept saying, "HE IS COMING...... THE KEYMAN IS COMING!"

CHAPTER SIX

I was in utter shock. Just a few minutes ago, Garry stood in front of me, perfectly fine and healthy, and next, he was on the ground, with a gigantic blade sticking right through the center of his throat. I didn't know what to do. There was a dead body lying in the doorway of my kitchen. I gagged, looking at the body on the ground. Panic started setting in. "What do I do now? If I call the cops, they will make sure that I go to jail, for how long, I don't know. What....what do I do?" I said as I paced throughout my kitchen, glancing at dead Garry from time to time. After a lot of thinking and pacing around, I knew what I had to do. I HAD TO PUT AN END TO THIS. That thing, whatever it was, has followed me from that hotel to my home. I could clearly remember Garry's last words, but I did not have a clue as to who or what the KEYMAN was. Then I suddenly realized what needed to be done, and when it did, I knew that I was an absolute genius. I would google it (In my defense, I just saw a man die right in front of me, and this is definitely all that came to mind.), which is what I was going to earlier before my house became a crime scene.

I carefully stepped out of the room, trying my level best not to step on Garry's body. (I still had no idea what to do about that body, but that did not seem as important at the moment). I immediately ran into my bedroom, where I had left my phone when I had gone to answer the door, and opened google. I immediately searched "Keyman," but all the results I found were definitely not related to anything that was happening with me. Now, the next best alternative I had was "Hotel Starlight." After scrolling through the google pages, I found nothing related to hotel starlight other than the location of that place. "Uugghh, what is wrong with you, google? You always have information on everything, then why nothing on a stupid hotel?" I said furiously as I kept scrolling through the various pages with links to everything except what I was looking for. Just as I reached the fourth-last search results page, my eyes fell upon a link that had the title that I was looking for. IT WAS A BLOG TITLED HOTEL STARLIGHT. I quickly clicked on that link, and it took me to the blog. It was written by a Siddharth Nahal. I was aware that I did not have much time, so I went straight into reading it.

"I entered the room and was not able to believe what I saw. I started sweating, and my knees felt weak. This room was very different from all other rooms in the hotel, it felt as if I had time traveled.

You are probably wondering what I am talking about. Let's go back in time a little bit, shall we?

I am JACK. I had lost my job due to the pandemic and was looking for jobs online. It was very hard to find a job because of the COVID-19 pandemic. As I was looking, I thought to myself "any job would be fine for now Jack, any job would be just fine", just then I stumbled upon an advertisement which read "Hotel Starlight, housekeeping wanted. Night shift position open. For more information regarding duties and salary call- 1122334455". I immediately picked up my phone and dialed the number. I spoke with the hotel manager and it was decided that I was to start work the next night.

It was my first time ever working a night shift so I wanted to prepare myself and sleep during the entire day before I went to work but that did not go according to plan. I was not able to get even an ounce of sleep the next day and drank three cups of coffee (I do not advise you to do that as it is probably not very healthy) before I left for my new job thinking that this might help me stay up all night. When I reached the hotel I saw what I was not expecting. I had imagined it to be a small ancient-looking hotel at the end of a street entirely secluded from every other building on the street. But in reality, the hotel was situated right in the middle of a row of fifteen houses and looked exactly like any other house on the street but had a small ancient board on the front gate that said "Hotel Starlight" in bold black letters. Upon going inside, I was told that there was a ground floor, a first floor, and three rooms on each floor. I was told to start work immediately. I was also told that there would be two people who would work in housekeeping.

After I finished all my chores, I sat down to take a break. All that coffee I had drank was definitely not helping me in any shape or form. While I was sitting, someone came up to me and sat down right next to me. We both started talking. I got to know that he was the other person hired for the housekeeping job. As we were talking the landline phone kept on the table next to me started ringing. I answered and a robot-like voice said "room number four" and the line got disconnected. I thought it was weird but knowing that this area had a lot of connection problems, I ignored it. The phone rang again after some time and this time the man's voice clearly said: "Please send a sandwich to room number four". As I kept the phone and told the other staff member that I was going to take a sandwich to room number four he said "the manager told me that room has been empty for years, there is no one staying there as it is sealed off, you must have made a mistake in hearing the room number". I told him that I heard the room number correct and that I was going to take the sandwich to that room. I got the order ready and took it to room number four.

As I reached the first floor I saw that the room door was wide open and a red light was coming from the room. I entered the room and was not able to believe what I saw. I started sweating and my knees felt weak. This room was very different from all other rooms in the hotel, it felt as if I had time traveled. The walls were covered in spider webs and dust, there was a thick layer of dust on the floor, bugs crawling everywhere and the room had a very ancient design and looked like a room from a king's palace. It had beautiful artwork covering the walls which were now covered in spider webs. It looked as if the room had been closed shut for thousands of years. I left the room at once and went straight to the manager. I told him everything that had happened and everything the other housekeeping said, still shaking. He told me that there was actually someone staying in that room for the past two weeks. Then he said, "you mentioned the other housekeeping, but nobody has been hired for that position yet. Could you tell me his name?". It was at this point I realized that I hadn't even asked him his name, and with that, I was told to take the order to room number four. When I went with the sandwich this time, there was a normal room there and someone staying in it. I delivered the order, apologized for the delay, and went back to the place where I was sitting earlier. My head was hurting thinking about everything that had happened earlier. Just then the manager called me to the front desk. I got up still a bit shaken from the incident and went to the front desk. When I reached there, the manager introduced me to someone, and I could not believe who it was. The manager said, "Jack, meet

Tom, he will be working with you as housekeeping". Standing in front of me was the other housekeeping staff I had met some time ago who told me about room number Four. Tom looked at me and said, "Are you okay? You look like you have seen a ghost".

WRITTEN BASED OFF OF THE ACCOUNTS GIVEN BY JACK."

That last line gave me the chills. "This can't be true, right? This could just be a work of fiction. If it was real, there would have been a mention of the so-called KEYMAN who Garry was talking about. No, I am not buying this. This has to be fake." I said as I looked around on the web page for any other information regarding this. Just then, I noticed another link right at the bottom of the page, titled- FALL OF THE STARLIGHT."

"FALL OF THE STARLIGHT." At this point, anything that contained starlight in it looked relevant to me, so I decided to open this link and read. This blog was also written by the same person as the one I read earlier. As I read this blog, shivers ran down my spine as I did not want to believe anything written in it. I did not want to believe even for a second that any of what was written here was true because nothing like this happened to me, and there was still no mention of THE KEYMAN. The blog went on like this-

"Have you ever been in a situation where you didn't know what was happening but were trying to make sense of it? That is the situation I am in now. I am Jack. You must remember me, right? I went to work at "Hotel Starlight," and some crazy stuff happened to me...... yes, I am that same person. You must have thought that everything was over after what had happened, right? I guess both of us were wrong there."

I know that this is a very generic start to any writeup to make it interesting, but what am I supposed to do? Whenever I hear or read the words HOTEL STARLIGHT anywhere, it gives me the chills. Anyways, the blog continued-

"The manager had called me to the front desk when I was thinking about everything that had happened to me. When I got there, he said, "Jack, meet Tom, he will be working with you as housekeeping." Standing in front of me was the other

housekeeping staff I had met some time ago who had told me about room number Four. Tom looked at me and said "Are you okay? You look like you have seen a ghost." Not knowing how to react to any of this, I replied "N...No, it's just been a long day." After that, I went on to do some more chores to keep myself occupied and not think about everything that had happened. After completing my work, I sat down to take a break, picked up one of the magazines kept in the waiting area, and started reading. It was a very old magazine and that was what had made me curious to read it. In that magazine, I found an advertisement that read, "Find all your answers in room number 4 at Hotel Starlight, it's the only way to escape. Avail while offer lasts." I read that out loud and the next thing I know, I am sitting on the ground, with my legs crossed, in room number Four.

I wanted to get up and leave immediately but I wasn't able to move, no, I didn't want to move. I couldn't help but notice the open magazine on my lap. The open page had the following written on it "Hotel Starlight, the place from where nobody ever returns. The only way to escape this place is to wait for the light of the star "ARCTURUS" to fall on the building which happens only once every nine years. The hotel becomes weak that night and cannot keep any human from leaving. The starlight will fall on the night of 31ˢᵗ of Quintilis 2021 at 3:30 AM." The paragraph was signed "T" at the end. Shaking with fear of everything that was happening, I tried to get up and was successful in doing so. I ran out of the room and went straight to the front desk but no one was there. I didn't want to believe anything I had read, so I went up to the front door and pulled on it as hard as I could.

Nothing happened. I tried again but wasn't able to open it. At this moment, I realized that being there was a huge mistake. I put my hand in my pocket to take out my phone *but it wasn't there. I must have dropped it on my way out of room number Four. I ran back upstairs and immediately went to room number Four. I saw my phone lying outside on the ground. I picked it up and found it completely smashed. Without wasting any time, I went back downstairs, only to realize that the whole time I had been busy running around all over the place in confusion and fear, I had not seen anyone. The manager, Tom, or any of the guests that were staying there. I knew that I had to find a way out. I remembered what the magazine said, "The date of the fall of the starlight is 31st of Quintilis 2021 at 3:30 AM", but what was Quintilis? As I was thinking about this, it struck me. In the ancient Roman calendar, the month of July was called Quintilis (I never thought that anything that we studied in school would help in saving my life someday) but wait a minute, today was the 31st of July. What a coincidence. It was almost 3:00 AM. I just had to survive in that place for thirty more minutes and I would be free. As I thought about this, I heard a voice coming from behind me.*

I turned around to see the manager standing there, with a sinister smile on his face. He looked directly into my eyes and said in a deep and raspy voice, "You cannot leave Jack. You belong to the hotel now." He slowly started to move towards me. All of a sudden it felt like I was falling from a twenty-floor high building. I landed with a thud on the ground and heard multiple voices say, "you cannot leave. You belong here with us now. I got up to see a very familiar-looking room. Yes, I was back in room number four. I ran to the door and tried opening it. I knew that this was it for me. I went to the middle of the room and sat down on the ground. There was nothing I could have done. I had accepted my fate. As I was sitting there, clueless as to what to do, I heard something ticking. I raised my head to see an ancient-looking clock on the wall right in front of me. The clock read 3:30 AM. All of a sudden the room door opened. I got up and ran outside. As I got out of the room, the entire building started shaking and water started filling the corridor. I quickly ran down the stairs, the water was at the level of my knees. As I reached the ground floor, someone grabbed my ankle and pulled me down. I went straight down into the water, completely submerged. I started panicking and somehow kicked my leg free from whoever was holding me down. I quickly started moving towards the front gate of the building, the water reached the level of my neck and the building had started to fall apart. Large chunks of the ceiling were falling. I moved as quickly as I could, trying to avoid everything that was falling. I reached the door and pulled as hard as I could. The door flew open and I was pushed out with all the water that had collected inside. I got up and ran outside the premises as fast as I could, completely soaked and gasping for air. The last thing I remember before everything went black was the entire hotel building falling apart into ruins.

That was three months ago. I have not been to that area since. It has been hard to forget everything that happened that night. Now I am supposed to go to the place where the hotel was for some work. As soon as I reached where the hotel was, I parked my car and got out to see what had happened to that place. I guess my curiosity got the best of me. I saw a ten-floor building there, something like a five-star hotel. Well, I was not wrong. It was indeed a five-star hotel and when I read the name on the newly painted board, I felt my stomach turn. The board said "WELCOME TO HOTEL STARLIGHT."

WRITTEN BASED OFF OF THE ACCOUNTS GIVEN BY JACK."

As soon as I finished reading this, I did not know what to think. After all the things that I had seen in that hotel, all of this also seemed believable. I was aware that whoever or whatever that weird man was, he was coming after me. I had to figure something out quickly. In order to be sure of some things related to that blog I just read, I went onto google and searched the word ARCTURUS, and there it was, all the required information on that star. I had a feeling that all of it was true after all. The only thing was that there was still no mention of the so-called KEYMAN anywhere. Just then, I remembered that I had read the name JACK somewhere else. Somewhere that was related to that hotel. I thought very hard about it, but I was not able to remember anything. I spent around twenty minutes pacing in my bedroom, trying to remember, and suddenly, it all came back to me. That one single review on the google location page for that eerie hotel. That review was by Jack. Without wasting any time, I quickly opened that page and went straight to the reviews section. I found the one review given by Jack, and when I did, I was utterly confused. The review was just a phone number. As thoughts raced through my head, trying to understand what was going on and make some very important decisions, I noticed a very pungent smell coming from somewhere (To be fair, so much was going on around me that I did indeed forget that there was a dead body lying in my kitchen doorway.), but I ignored it as all of my focus went towards one single question, "SHOULD I CALL THE GIVEN PHONE NUMBER OR NOT?"

CHAPTER EIGHT

After a lot of thought, I decided to call that number. I got a little nervous, and my hands started shaking (fine, I admit that it was not nervousness but fear, as I still had hopes for it to all be a hallucination for me). I doubted whether anyone would pick up because that review was from four years ago. The first time no one picked up, but on the second attempt, I got a response. The voice sounded mature, old, and concerned. "Hello, who is this?" the voice on the other end asked. "J....Jack?" I responded in a shaky voice. The voice on the other end said, "You went to the hotel, didn't you?" As soon as I heard that, chills ran down my spine. How in the world did he even know that? I slowly started narrating what had happened to me, but it was hard to articulate it in words.

After listening to me, he told me about what happened to him there. He verified that those blogs' facts were true and how he knew that I had visited the hotel. He said, "I was there as well, exactly in the same situation you are now. I know what kind of fear that place brings out in people. I know what it's like to be in a situation where no one is ready to believe anything you say related to that hotel. Most people are not even able to see it." I then asked him about the so-called KEYMAN, and he said that he would tell me everything, but I needed to be a bit patient. He offered to help me, and when I asked him, "Not to be rude, but why would you help a stranger with a thing that is definitely life-threatening?" To this, he responded calmly, "I have lost the people who were closest to me because of the demon present there, and it would be disrespectful to them if I do not help someone experiencing the same situation I experienced four years ago." I did not feel like asking him about what happened to his loved ones, but I had to clarify some things. I immediately asked, "Demon? There is a demon in that place?"

His reply to this question was, "Yes, all that is happening to you is caused by that demon." I was very confused, but at this point, nothing seemed hard to believe. I blurted out, "How do you know all this? What happened with you after you escaped that place? According to what I am aware of, you destroyed that place, so how is it still there, and why is that thing after me?" as soon as he heard my questions, he said, "I will tell you everything in person. Just know that that demon does not remain confined to the hotel itself. Every person that enters room number four is that demon's victim, and once it is done with that victim, it will go after everyone the victim cares about. In my case, the light from the star destroyed the hotel and saved me, but in your case, that is not possible, at least for the next five years, so you need to be very careful because that demon has attached itself to you, and it won't stop until it fills your and your loved ones' lives with sorrow and pain before ending it entirely." he took a short pause and said," Meet me right outside the hotel in an hour."

Before I could say anything, the line disconnected, and I was left with many questions, stress, and an immense amount of fear. I was not even sure if this was really Jack. As I sat there thinking about this, I realized that my entire bedroom was filled with a very pungent smell that almost made me puke. I had genuinely forgotten that there was a dead body lying in my house, which had definitely started to decompose. I knew that I had to leave, but I had to dispose of Garry's body because it being found in my apartment would lead to the generation of a huge load of trouble for me.

Without wasting another second, I got up and went straight to where the body was lying, and as soon as I saw it, I threw up. It was definitely the most horrendous sight I had ever seen, and it definitely topped that room full of bodies I saw earlier. Garry's body lay right there, entirely pale, the blood on his neck had dried up, forming a thick crusty layer around the blade sticking through, making it look like it had been sealed in with a layer of red-colored cement. There was another slimy-looking liquid forming around the majority of the wounds. I was sure that it was pus. The skin hanging from various places had completely dried up, still attached to the body, and his lifeless eyes looked straight up. As I got closer to the body, it started smelling worse. The worst part was about to begin now. I had to somehow move the body and get it out of my apartment building without people noticing and then go ahead and dispose of it in a place where nobody finds it. Not really knowing what I was doing, I found a pair of old gloves and wore them to ensure that my fingerprints did not get on the body, just like killers did in the movies while disposing of the body of their victims. I had a clear plan in mind, just like in the movies, I would take the body out to the nearest forest, and within its depths, I would bury it so deep in the ground that nobody would ever find it. I grabbed the body from under its arms, slowly lifting the upper half off the ground. What made it extremely difficult, apart from the smell, was the fact that Garry was simply way too heavy for me, and his body had become so stiff and cold. I slowly and with much effort dragged his body straight to my front door. I felt so disgusted as the pus in his body got onto my hands. As I was about to open the front door of my apartment, the bell to my house rang.

I jumped up from this loud sound and dropped the body straight to the ground. I looked through the peephole in the door and saw a delivery person standing outside. I opened the door, only enough for my voice to go outside, and told the delivery person to leave the package outside. Once he was gone, I closed the door and took a huge sigh of relief. For a moment, I had forgotten what I was doing. I immediately got right back at getting the body out of my apartment. It did not take me very long to get the body out of the building, as, at night, the building looked abandoned, as if no one ever lived there. As soon as I got the body in the underground parking where my bike was parked, I realized two things. First, I had left Garry's phone in my apartment, and second, I did not think this through. How was I going to carry him on a bike without being noticed? Just as I was thinking about this, I realized what to do. I immediately dragged the body to a corner of the parking where it won't be visible to anyone easily and ran back up to my apartment to get the biggest and the only travel bag I had. It was an old cloth bag, which was missing one of its two wheels but it had worked for me for so many years and was going to today as well, for the very last time. I grabbed the bag as fast as I could, along with the first piece of cloth I found, which turned out to be a t-shirt, to cover my nose, and went straight down to the parking. I carefully scanned the area for any people before I approached the body. I covered my nose with the t-shirt, which worked very well in keeping the terrible smell of decay out, and started stuffing the body in the bag.

The best part about this building was that it was very old, so there were no CCTV cameras which made my job easier and more convenient. The bag was big enough to accommodate the body somehow, but the only problem was due to the body being stiff. This made it hard for me to accommodate the limbs in the bag. I had to force them in, in the process of which I heard a few bones snap, which made me gag. As soon as I was done stuffing the body in the bag, I somehow managed to balance the bag as I slowly drove my bike to a forest that was only a few kilometers away. I trekked through the uneven grounds of the forest, struggling as I pulled the heavy bag with one hand and shone my phone's flashlight into the dark forest grounds with the other. Once I was deep inside, I found a strong enough stick lying around and started digging. It took me a while to dig a deep enough hole since I had no tools to do so (See, I truly didn't think this through). I dumped the bag into the hole and covered it in such a way that it easily blended with the environment. I was panting and sweating profusely and decided to sit for a minute because this was a lot for me.

CHAPTER NINE

As I sat down, right next to where I had buried the body, I thought of what was happening to me and what I was doing because of it. "I should have never gone to that hotel. I am sorry, Garry." I said softly as I looked down at where the body was. I took my phone out to check the time. An hour and a half had passed since I talked to Jack or whoever that was, and my phone was full of missed calls from his number. I called him back, and as soon as he picked the call up, he asked, "WHERE ARE YOU? I have been waiting for you outside the hotel for the past thirty minutes." I replied, "Sorry about that; I had something important to take care of. I will be there in fifteen minutes." I cut the call and got up to leave, which is when I heard it. My name. "David........David." It sounded like a wounded person was whispering right next to my ear. I looked around and flashed the flashlight from my phone, but there was no one in sight.

I started walking fast towards the area where I had left my bike, which is when I saw a figure standing behind one of the trees to my right. I turned to look in that direction, but no one was there. I started walking even faster than before, struggling to light the path in front of me. The problem was that the forest was so dark at night that nothing was really visible. After a few minutes of going towards my bike, or at least I thought I was going towards my bike, I tripped on something and fell face first. As I slowly got up, flinching from a pain that rose in my nose, I picked my phone up, which was perfectly fine somehow, and as I touched my nose to check if it was bleeding or not, I saw a thick, red liquid on my hand under the phone's flashlight. I took the t-shirt I had used to cover my nose earlier and used it to press against my nose in an attempt to stop the bleeding. I turned around to look at what I had tripped on, but nothing was clearly visible. I immediately pointed my phone's flashlight In that direction, and the light fell on Garry's lifeless body lying on the ground. As soon as I saw that, chills ran up my spine. How was that possible? I had just buried the body deep inside the ground. At that exact moment, I heard a loud twig breaking sound right behind me. I immediately spun around and pointed the light in that direction, only to see what I feared the most.

The man with the stitches in place of lips stood there, his lifeless eyes staring straight into mine, extending the burnt hand in which he held the keys as if offering the keys to me. I immediately turned around and darted straight through the forest and reached the area where I had parked my bike. As I sat on the bike, the weird man appeared right in front of me and touched a glowing red key to my forehead. I felt sadness and pain as everything around me started feeling gloomy. The intensity of the pain increased so much that I screamed as loud as possible. As I sat on my bike, not knowing what to do, I heard that whisper again. The voice said, "I can relieve you from this pain. I can make sure that you never feel any pain ever again. Just take this key from me, and I promise that you will NEVER FEEL PAIN OR SORROW EVER AGAIN." As the intensity of the pain grew, I couldn't take it anymore. So, I did what I had to do. I slowly raised my hand and grabbed the key, and as soon as I did, all the pain and suffering went away. I felt so amazing. It felt as if nothing bad could ever happen to me again. Just then, I heard that voice again, "David, Welcome to Hotel Starlight. I am happy to have you as my helper. Now, we shall do what is necessary. Go back to the hotel, and get Jack inside the building." I don't know what happened to me, but I knew exactly what the weird man wanted, I mean, I knew exactly what the keyman wanted, and I knew what I had to do to make sure that he got it. The keyman helped me and saved me from all the pain and suffering, how could I not help him?

CHAPTER TEN

I reached the hotel in about half an hour and called Jack. He told me he was waiting for me in his car, which was a good old dodge challenger. I located the car and opened the door to the seat right next to the driver's. I sat in and took a long good look at Jack. His appearance did not match my expectations at all. I thought that he would be a middle-aged man with a big bushy beard and tired-looking eyes, but it turned out to be the complete opposite. Jack was a young man, probably in his late twenties, who looked as lively as one could be. He looked at me and said, "What took you so long? You made me wait for about two full hours outside this 5-star nightmare. Where were you? What happened? You look like you have seen a ghost." Just as he said this, I blurted out everything that had happened to me, "My boss died in my apartment because of the keyman, and I had to go to the most awful thing to get rid of his body, and when I was doing so, the keyman came after me. I barely made it out of that forest."

To this, he calmly responded, "It's all right. You are fine, at least for now. Anyways, this demon I told you about, he can make things happen. Really bad things.' He took a long pause after saying this and then continued, "The time I used to work here, which was not a long time ago, around four years, when all you read about in that blog happened to me, I was not aware that there was a demon there. The demon, who used to be the manager of the hotel in his human form, grew weak after the hotel got destroyed by the starlight of the star Arcturus. You see, what you saw was the true form of that demon. Anyways, where was I? Right, the demon was growing weaker. So, after I got out, I started seeing him, in his true form now, around my house, around my neighborhood, and any other place I went to, which is when I decided to find out what was really going on with me. There was no mention of it on the internet anywhere, so I went to a few libraries, and after going to the oldest one I could possibly locate, I found it. One very old book on everything ranging from black magic to demons." He took a short pause and looked a bit hesitant to give further information, which is why I asked him, "So, what did you find in the book?" He looked at me as if I had asked the only question he was hoping I would not ask. He took a deep breath and said, "It mentioned something about an ancient entity, known by many names over the years, the most recent one being the KEYMAN. It is said that this entity feeds off of fear. It also mentioned that it is caught in a vicious cycle. A cycle that repeats itself every nine years, and when it does, the hotel gets destroyed, and the KEYMAN becomes weak." I immediately interjected him by saying, "Does that mean we can end it once and for all?" He looked at me with concerned eyes, and ignoring my question, continued talking. "It lives by taking people's souls and possessing the bodies of the ones that show little to no fear for it. It possesses the fearless ones and lives on in that body till it's time for the starlight to fall on the hotel. You see, David, the starlight is what makes him weak, and when it does, that entity has to leave the body that it had possessed, taking that person's soul with it. It then looks for a new host, and I am sorry, but it looks like it has chosen you as his next host."

I was not able to comprehend any of the things he had said. I slowly responded, "No.......It can't be. I am just a normal SCARED person who used to work at a small restaurant, that's it. I am pretty sure that you are mistaken. It can't.......be me. You are mi.....mistaken. There is no way it's me. I am definitely the most scared person on this planet. It is definitely not me. Think about what your sister would say if she was here. Even she would know that it can't be me, after all, she had encountered this entity that ended up killing her, remember, and she was definitely more fearless than me" As soon as I said that last line, he looked at me as if I had said something that I shouldn't have, and I was definitely getting a punch right to the nose, but the thought that what the keyman wanted would occur filled me with a subtle feeling of joy. A minute passed as we sat there in silence, which was broken when I opened the car door and got out, and told Jack that we needed to hurry and go inside as the only way to figure out how to stop that thing before it got to me. He got out of the car and said, "How are you so sure that we will find a way to end this all inside this hotel? As far I am aware, the only way to end this is if the starlight falls on this hotel again, but that is not going to happen for the next five years." To this, I responded with a huge smile, "Trust me, I just have a good feeling about this."

Both of us headed straight through the entrance of the beautifully built hotel, and Jack mentioned that the layout of the hotel was the exact same as before but more modernized and expensive looking. He told me that we should start looking from one of the rooms on the ground floor, which was a closet. The closet door had keys hanging in the lock for some reason. I peeked inside the door to see if something was wrong, which is when I felt a hard push from behind, which sent me straight into the closet. I turned around and saw the door close. As soon as the door closed, I ran up to it and yanked at the handle as hard as possible, but it didn't budge. I screamed and called Jack as I tried to open the door, "Jack, help me. The door isn't opening. Jaaaaaaaack, Help!" I hit the door as hard as possible in an attempt to get it open, which is when I heard Jack's voice. "It got to you, didn't it?" He asked as I stopped hitting the door. "What are you talking about? Open the door, Jack. JUST OPEN THE DOOR AND LET ME OUT OF HERE." I said as anger took over me. He immediately responded, "No. He got to you before we could find a way to end this, and do you know how I know about this? The very minute you mentioned my sister's death with such detail. I never mentioned anything about my sister's death to you, and I know for a fact that those fictitious blogs definitely don't." As soon as I heard this, it felt as if I had something in a previously empty pocket of my jeans. I put my hand into my pocket to find a key there, Glowing red, which helped me to open the door.

I slowly walked out of the closet, looking straight at Jack and smiling. "You are very smart, Jack. See, the thing is that the keyman showed me the true and best way to stay alive forever, without any pain and suffering. This cruel world will not let anyone live for long, let alone me and you, but the KEYMAN will change all that." Jack cut me off as I spoke and said, "What did that thing do to you?" I looked at him, with a disgusted look in my eyes, and said, "That thing? Come on, Jack. Show some respect, he has a name. Also, for your information, he showed me all the pain and suffering that my future has in store for me and helped me escape it and live on forever. Anyways, enough about me.

Let's talk about YOU now. What he truly wants is YOU. He always has. When he met me in the forest, he made me understand the importance of getting you to this hotel, and since he helped me, I decided to help him. You know he needs a new body, right? Well, that body has to be yours, and he is at his strongest in this hotel, which is why he needed me to bring you here so that he can possess that precious body of yours and live on. Aahhh, here he comes." I could clearly see Jack's expression change from confusion to sorrow, and he looked like he was about to cry. "It's okay, Jack. He will liberate you from all this pain and sadness too."

I turned around to see the KEYMAN standing there. He slowly moved forward until he was right in front of Jack. As he moved forward, I could clearly see the broken bone sticking out of his thigh move in a slow but continuous motion, as it went in when he straightened his leg and came out when he bent his knee. I went ahead and moved right behind Jack so that I could clearly see the KEYMAN; after all, he had helped me so much, and I felt indebted to him. Just at that moment, Jack got up and tried to run, which is when I had to, unwillingly, punch him straight on the nose, which made him fall back to the ground. As he held his bleeding nose, he crawled towards the keyman, looked straight in his eyes, and exclaimed, "You will never get what you want, you filthy demon!" As I was about to grab Jack and punch him again for what he had just said, I heard a loud ripping noise. I looked up at the keyman and saw the stitches on his mouth ripping open one by one. It was not a pleasant sight to look at. I could clearly see the destroyed teeth through the lipless mouth, from which streams of blood flowed as all the stitches ripped open one by one. Through this destroyed mouth, a feeble voice said, "Can you feel it, Jack? All that pain and suffering." Large droplets of blood flew in every direction as these words came out of the keyman's mouth. Suddenly, Jack started wincing and screaming in pain. The keyman continued, "Take the keys, Jack, let me liberate you from this pain. You are the mo- the most fearless person I have encountered in the past decade. You not only managed to escape me, but you managed to escape this hotel when it was getting demolished. Since then, I knew that you were destined to be my next host. Oh, I have dreamt of you, I have missed you so much. Haven't you as well? Now give me control of your body Jack, and I shall ensure that you never feel this pain again. Together, we can thrive forever. LET ME LIBERATE YOU, JACK. LET ME LIBERATE YOU." The keyman extended the burnt hand holding the hinged ring with keys on it as if offering them to Jack. As Jack screamed in pain, I could see his hand slowly extend to grab the keys.

That was four months ago. Now, I work at the hotel, and honestly, it has been a blast. I also have my own room here, room number four. Life is great. No more pain, suffering, or fear of any kind. JUST A GOOD LIFE. The keyman is also healthy as ever, and as long as he thrives, we here at THE HOTEL NAMED STARLIGHT, thrive till eternity.

THE END

Afterword

Hello, I hope you liked the story and had a fun time reading it. Thank you for reading this book!

If you want to read any short stories written by me, then scan the QR code given below-

About The Author

Siddharth Nahal was born in Delhi, India, in the year 2003. He is an Economics student currently residing and studying in Bangalore. He has always been fascinated by the world of the supernatural and has written multiple short stories related to it. Other than writing, he is passionate about martial arts. The Hotel Named Starlight is Siddharth's first book.